TO VANISHING POINT

When Hazel looked out of the window at school and saw a strange silver girl looking back at her – she couldn't believe her eyes. Who was the silver girl? What did she want and where did she come from? Why could no-one else see her? And what was causing the strange glow in the playground?

Doreen Norman

To Vanishing Point

Illustrated by John Hutchinson

CAROUSEL EDITOR: ANNE WOOD

TRANSWORLD PUBLISHERS LTD
A National General Company

TO VANISHING POINT

A CAROUSEL BOOK 0 552 52003 9

First publication in Great Britain

PRINTING HISTORY
Carousel edition published 1971

Copyright © Doreen Norman 1971
Illustrations copyright © Transworld Publishers Ltd., 1971

Carousel Books are published by Transworld Publishers Ltd.,
Cavendish House, 57–59 Uxbridge Road, Ealing, London W.5.
Made and printed in Great Britain by
Hazell Watson & Viney Ltd., Aylesbury, Bucks

for
Carolann and Katharine

CHAPTER ONE

"It must be my reflection," Hazel said to herself. She had finished her arithmetic before the other children and was staring at the classroom window.

All day the October mist had clung about the town, hiding the sun. Mr. Thomas had switched on the classroom lights and the inside of the windows gleamed.

Hazel's cousin Simon nudged her elbow and she looked away from the face in the glass.

Simon whispered, "Have you finished?" He was twisting his red hair round his fingers.

Hazel pushed her book across carefully, so that it could be seen from both their desks. Simon began to write feverishly and Hazel looked back at the window.

The reflection was strange. It had Hazel's soft features and brown hair, but when she moved her head the face in the window stayed still. Hazel experimented by touching her hair, but no hand moved to touch the reflection's hair.

"I hope you've got it right," Simon muttered as he pushed back Hazel's book.

Hazel hardly noticed. She stared at the face and pulled back her lips as though in a smile. The face was quite unmoved. Reflections should not behave like that and Hazel frowned at this one.

"When Hazel Bradley has finished scowling at

the window," Mr. Thomas said, "we'll have the
books passed up in an orderly fashion." His look
rested severely on Hazel, so that she dared not return her attention to the window yet.

In an absent-minded way, Hazel pushed her
glasses higher up on her nose and a thought ran

through her like iced water. The reflection had no glasses.

Hazel's curiosity became almost unbearable as she searched in her untidy desk for the English book. When Mr. Thomas turned to write on the blackboard, Hazel twisted her head towards the window. The face was still there, but the features had become blurred.

Before Hazel's startled eyes the face moved along the window, where it was impossible for her own reflection to look back at her, with or without glasses. Slowly the face rose as the owner stretched to stand on tiptoe. The hair changed to a shimmering silver and the features became clear again.

It was quite a different face. The nose, lips and chin were very delicate, but the cheekbones were wide. The shoulders below the face were covered with what Hazel thought must be a dull, silver satin.

Hazel's true reflection and the silver creature both gazed through the window. The silver creature had large eyes that watched Hazel without blinking.

Hazel felt her throat become tight, just as it did when she saw the first tinselled Christmas tree each year. She was almost glad when Mr. Thomas said, "Tell me about verbs, Simon."

There was a pause, during which Mr. Thomas tapped a piece of chalk on his table. Simon scuffled his feet and, in the careful whisper she had developed Hazel said, "Doing."

Simon said, "They're 'doing' words, sir."

Mr. Thomas turned and began to write on the blackboard.

"Look at the window, Simon," Hazel whispered.

Simon's head swivelled in the direction of the face, remained briefly and then came back as Mr. Thomas fired a question at Duncan who sat in the back row.

"Well?" Hazel asked.

"Stop messing about," Simon whispered. "There's only a few dead old leaves."

Simon must surely have seen, Hazel thought. The autumn leaves were falling and a handful drifted in an irregular red and gold pattern on to the silver shoulders. Hazel sighed wistfully. Someone was not in school, someone was free to scrunch through the leaves.

"Are you nutty today?" Simon asked, as he leaned across Hazel's desk to borrow a pencil. She shook her head.

"I shall separate you Bradley children if this whispering continues," Mr. Thomas said. He had begun to mark exercise books and this always seemed to make him irritable.

With some difficulty, Hazel turned her eyes away from the window and bent over her English book. She longed for school to end so that she could find out more about the silver creature, but the big hand of the classroom clock crept round.

When Mr. Thomas at last dismissed the class, there was the usual huddle of pushing boys in the doorway and the girls straggled behind. Hazel went across to the window and moved along until she was level with the face. How could someone stay so long in one position, she wondered?

The silver creature backed away. Although the silver hair was very short, Hazel could tell from the creature's way of moving that it was a girl – a girl in a closely fitting silvery suit of tunic and trousers.

Schoolchildren who had scrambled early through the cloakrooms began to spill into the playground. The silver-suited girl moved swiftly, in a glide rather than a run, towards the most distant corner. The autumn leaves gathered up from the ground and swept down from the trees to make a cascade about her.

The girl stooped. Hazel stared at the spot. The girl had disappeared.

When Hazel came out from the school building, the playground was empty except for Simon, Duncan and John. Hazel walked towards the boys.

Duncan had a sharply curved, blue plastic toy in his hand. They all examined it.

"It's not like a proper boomerang," John said.

"It's as good as. It'll come back if you throw it the right way," Duncan said proudly. "Watch."

He held the boomerang lightly. He raised his arm and moved it swiftly. But the boomerang flew to one side and clattered on the ground a few yards away. Simon and John both laughed.

Duncan's face flushed pink. "You have to get the knack," he said.

Hazel sighed. She was sure they would mock if she told them about the silver-suited girl. They would tease her about her glasses. And this test of

the boomerang might take some time; until Duncan made it work, or a teacher sent them home.

Hazel drifted towards the spot where she had last seen the girl. Curiosity drew her nearer and yet her feet dragged. Before she reached the place, Hazel put down her schoolbag and sat on it. The bundle of gym clothes in the bag made a cushiony seat.

She thought about the silver girl and stared at the now empty corner, her back to the boys. The girl had seemed so real and yet Simon had not seen. Hazel wondered if sharing the secret would help her to understand the puzzle.

The boomerang came flying past. Hazel saw it as a blur that moved rapidly in the direction of the high playground wall.

As it moved, Duncan shouted, "It'll work this time!"

"No, it'll hit the wall!" John cried.

But the boomerang did neither of these things. Near the corner of the playground its flight stopped suddenly and the boomerang remained quite still in mid-air. Then it vanished.

"Again!" Hazel cried out in excitement. A girl had vanished, a boomerang had vanished, both in exactly the same place; and she, shortsighted Hazel Bradley, had seen both things happen.

The three boys ran across shouting.

CHAPTER TWO

"Where's it gone?" Duncan said. He looked at the wall. "It could have lifted up and gone over."

"That's daft," Simon said, "we'd have seen."

Duncan kicked a few loose leaves and then bent down. "We could look through these."

The boys began to turn the leaves over. Hazel watched them. The leaves were scattered too far apart to hide a blue plastic boomerang, but she said nothing. The boys should be able to see that. And they had been watching the boomerang's flight, they must have seen it disappear into nowhere.

As he kicked through the leaves, Duncan approached the corner. He staggered and almost lost his balance. He steadied himself, rubbed his shoulder and looked about him angrily. Hazel saw his mouth open as though he was going to shout.

"Somebody pushed. . . ." Duncan began, but his mouth remained open.

With Simon trailing behind him, John had come over to Hazel. "Did you see where it went, Hazel?" John asked.

Before Hazel could answer, Duncan said, "Maybe *she* picked it up and threw it over the wall." He came towards them, still rubbing his shoulder.

"It just disappeared," Hazel said.

"Things don't just disappear," Duncan said. "I bet she's got it."

"No one's got it, so shut up!" Simon shook his head so that his red hair stood up in an unruly mass. His usually pale face turned pink between the freckles.

There was silence for a moment as the children stood in a downcast group, carefully not looking at each other. Then from behind them Mr. Thomas' voice said, "Time you were out of here."

Duncan faced the spindly-looking Mr. Thomas and lifted his chin. "My boomerang's been pinched," he said.

"Then the less you say about it the better, Duncan Wright," Mr. Thomas said, "boomerangs are weapons and you know the school rule. And Simon Bradley and John Crofts would do well to remember it as well."

Hazel heard Duncan raise his voice defiantly in answer and wondered how he could. To ease her awkward feeling she looked away towards the corner. Duncan must have been at least seven or eight feet away from the wall when he staggered.

She took off her glasses and wiped them with her handkerchief. Without the glasses everything misted into a blur of soft colours and shapes.

Although the playground wall was now merely a fuzzy yellow, Hazel still knew exactly where the corner was. She thought she saw a dim shape, a slight movement. She held out her hand and walked slowly towards the shape.

The movement and the shape went in the way that a picture flickers when a television set is switched off. There was a slight click and Hazel's hand jerked back. She stopped, uncertain whether she did not want to move on or whether something was preventing her.

"Old Thomas has gone. Come on, Hazel!" Simon pulled at her sleeve. In a quieter voice he said, "You've broken your specs."

Hazel peered. The lenses were unharmed, but the frames were broken at one side. She would not be able to wear them.

"They're your new specs," Simon said. "Aunt Edna'll be wild."

"I didn't drop them," Hazel said. "They were in my hand. I just bumped against something – then they went click."

"Try that one on Aunt Edna," Simon said.

Hazel believed that on an ordinary day she would have found it hard not to cry about her broken glasses. But today things were far from ordinary and she stood there in wonder.

"Are you coming?" John called.

Hazel could see John as a navy blue blur by the playground arch. Simon steered her towards him. "You won't get knocked down with us," he said.

"I can see *shapes* without them, and read too," Hazel said sharply. Because she wore glasses it did not mean that she could not see anything without them. She just saw a different world. She walked through her different world with Simon on one side and John on the other.

"Duncan Wright's a blooming twit," Simon said suddenly, after they had left the school grounds and crossed the main road.

"Mum doesn't like you to talk like that," Hazel said, though secretly she thought Simon's cockney-tinged slang was very expressive.

"They say worse on the telly," Simon said.

"Duncan is a twit, anyway," John said. "He thinks you pinched his boomerang, Hazel. Marvo the Magician, that's you!"

"Well, she hasn't," Simon said. "We couldn't have a proper look with old Thomas snooping."

"It must have dropped somewhere without us seeing," John said. "We could meet up after tea and have another look."

"And after lousy homework, you mean," Simon said grimly.

"That will be another fifteen shillings to pay out," Mrs. Bradley said as she turned the sausages briskly in the frying pan.

Hazel sat at the kitchen table and nodded at her mother as if to imply that she understood all about such matters of finance. The broken glasses lay on the table and the old glasses were tight across her nose.

"I can't imagine how you came to break them just walking along," Mrs. Bradley said. She speared the sausages and slipped them on to a plate which she then placed in the oven. "Tea's almost ready. You'd best tell Simon."

Hazel wondered how one began to explain about disappearing girls and vanishing boomerangs, how Duncan had been pushed and her own glasses broken by something that was not there to be seen.

She decided not to try. She closed her school books and put them in a neat pile on the hatchway to the living room.

"Not there, Hazel," her mother said. "I'll be putting the plates through soon. Hurry up, if you're going to get to Guides on time tonight."

Hazel trailed upstairs with her books. She put them on the chair in her bedroom and then went to see Simon.

Simon sat on his bed, gloomily staring at his history book. The chapter of "Portrait of the Middle Ages" had to be read before he would be allowed to watch television or go out.

Hazel stood in the open doorway. Simon's was the smallest bedroom, but Mr. Bradley had fitted it up well. "Our home's your cousin's home now," Mr. Bradley had explained when Simon had come to live with them last year.

There was a pegboard on which Simon pinned his pictures of racing cars, and a shelf fitment for his toolkit and model aeroplanes.

Hazel touched one of the models. She liked the sleek smoothness of the lines. She knew that there was a parcel already hidden away for Simon's Christmas present – a kit for making a model of the Concorde. Hazel wished people would give her model kits instead of embroidery sets. Then she thought of the adults' hushed voices when Simon's parents were mentioned, of the months Simon had spent in a council home after his grandmother died.

She took her hand from the model aeroplane and said, "Tea's ready."

Simon closed the book with a firm bang and a loud sigh of relief.

They heard the thud of the front door as Mr. Bradley came in from work. He 'hallooed' up the stairs and then went into the kitchen, where his low tones blended with Mrs. Bradley's higher voice.

"That'll be about your specs," Simon said.

"Don't you think it odd, Simon?" Hazel asked, trying to put her words carefully. "About my glasses and the boomerang? I mean, both in almost the same place."

"Your specs didn't do a vanishing trick."

"Yes, but the boomerang did. And my glasses – it was as though I'd walked into a wall that was there and yet wasn't."

Simon laughed. He said, "You wouldn't see it with your specs off, would you?"

"But I wasn't anywhere near the wall when you came over, was I?" Hazel said. She saw Simon's forehead crease thoughtfully.

Mrs. Bradley called them from the kitchen and the children went down the stairs.

In the hall, Simon said, "You ought to come and have another dekko with John and me."

"It's Guides," Hazel said.

"Skip the blooming Guides, then," Simon said.

CHAPTER THREE

"Perhaps you dreamt it," John said to Hazel.

Simon and Hazel had met John by the chemist's shop in the High Street. The three children now stood by the school gate in the growing twilight.

Hazel felt better now that she had told Simon and John how she had seen the silver girl disappear. But she felt strangely nervous about re-entering the playground. Simon and John seemed as hesitant as she was.

"Might've been a ghost," Simon said speculatively.

"In broad daylight!" John said. He swaggered through the gate in a daredevil way, only to stop as soon as he was inside. "Come on then, let's *all* go and have a look."

"It's not broad daylight now," Simon said, as he and Hazel followed slowly.

The school was on the outskirts of the town, where the wind whipped across flat fields. The mist of the day had blown away and, beyond the playing fields, the yellow-brick school buildings shone garishly against the grey dusk. Lights were on in one of the classrooms.

"That'll be the caretaker," John said.

They started off towards the brick wall that enclosed the playground. Lights began to shine weakly in the streets that bordered the eastern side of the school.

"Soon be dark," Hazel said.

"We must be a bit touched to come." Simon's voice trembled.

Hazel said, "The girl didn't look like a ghost, she was different but too . . . solid." She spoke partly to reassure the boys and partly to give herself courage.

"How do you know what a ghost *does* look like?" John asked.

The children stood on the far side of the playground and studied what they could see of the corner in the half-light. The wind rustled the fallen leaves across the ground.

"I've got my torch," Simon said.

John laughed in an uneasy way. "I don't suppose a torch would be any good against a ghost."

Hazel felt that they were wasting time. She pressed her lips firmly together and approached the corner. For a moment she stood at a loss: what was she looking for?

Then she half-knelt. It was still light enough for her to see the scattered leaves. They appeared to make a curving line. The line marked a wide quarter-circle in the corner which was completely free of leaves.

Some leaves were propelled towards the corner. They never reached it. The wind made them quiver in mid-air, as though it blew them against a window. When the wind changed course, the leaves dropped and scattered.

"Something *is* there," Hazel whispered. She wondered why the leaves had not vanished as the boomerang had done. Some things vanished, like the silver girl and the boomerang; some things were pushed away, like Duncan, her glasses and the leaves.

The boys' slow footsteps sounded across the playground. Simon called, "Found anything?"

Hazel straightened up and put her hand where she thought the leaves had been held back in the air. She could not move her hand forward.

"Wait!" John shouted. "It's almost dark enough for the torch."

Hazel turned. It was very nearly dark now, but she could just see Simon and John as hazy figures coming closer. She did not know what happened next. One moment she was waving, the next moment she was drawn backwards.

The playground and the night sky disappeared. Hazel's breath left her body. She became extremely hot. Her body felt twice its usual size. There was a great pressure that Hazel thought would last for ever. She opened her mouth to scream soundlessly that she could not bear it.

Then the pressure collapsed about her. Hazel was pushed against a hard metallic surface. The surface slid away from her and she fell dizzily.

Gradually the heat lessened. Hazel could breathe again. Her body felt its normal size. Slight images moved. Hazel felt at her face to make sure her glasses were still there. She could see again, but what had happened?

She was in a shadowy darkness, that was yet not quite darkness. Everything that was not black had a reddish glow. There were strong, black shapes, less distinct purple and crimson shapes.

A few feet away stood a small, vague figure. The figure seemed to change substance, at one moment appearing to Hazel half-transparent, at the next quite solid.

A sound came from the figure. The sound was fast and very high in pitch. It could hardly be described as words, Hazel thought, yet it was certainly a voice.

The voice stopped. There was a pause and it began again. This time it was pitched lower, but Hazel still could not pick out any words. She shook her head in bewilderment.

The vague figure moved forward a little. It gave a deep sigh. It seemed to be peering at Hazel.

Then, at last, it said, slowly and distinctly:

"I landed on the wrong planet."

CHAPTER FOUR

"I was on a mission from Alpha Centauri A to Epsilon Eridanus," said the shadowy figure.

"What is this place?" Hazel said.

"My ship's auto-pilot has failed," said the figure, "and the matter transmission system is not working correctly. When the force field weakens my ship will become completely visible."

It was warm in the place and the figure wavered in the unearthly reddish light. Was this some strange underworld, Hazel wondered? Was this figure a ghost? If it was a ghost, it surely must be playing a joke.

Hazel said, "Please tell me why I'm here."

The figure said, "I am in great difficulty. My people's mission is vital and it cannot be completed without me."

"I suppose you've taken the silver girl off too?" Hazel said.

"Silver girl?" said the figure. There was a pause. "Ah!"

The figure moved away. A switch clicked. The warmth lessened. The reddish glow changed to pink and gradually the light became paler, a golden white.

"*You're* the silver girl!" Hazel said.

The silver girl turned away from a large panel that ran across one curving wall. She smiled at

Hazel "I forgot your people would not be able to see properly in the infra-red."

Hazel stared around her. The dark-coloured shapes had changed. There were two chairs fixed to the floor, a screen that partly divided the area in half and two bunks set in one wall. The ceiling and floor were slightly curved and gleaming.

What had the girl said, Alpha Centauri A? Hazel had never heard of it. She decided it must be some outlandish place.

The silver girl sat in one of the chairs. All her movements had a liquid flow and now she twisted her limbs one about the other in an extraordinary fashion. She lifted her face and the large eyes, more like crystals than of any colour, looked hopefully at Hazel.

Behind the girl a panel gave out a constant murmuring vibration. Lights flashed across it in ripples.

"The mentor is quite disorientated since the transmission equipment went wrong," the girl said as though that explained everything.

Hazel said, "What's it all about? Why have you brought me in here? You did bring me in, I suppose?"

"I thought you came to help," said the girl, "that's why I invited you in. You give out a different, brighter beam than the others, so it was obvious you would understand. Think what it's like when your auto-pilot *and* the transmission equipment fails!"

Infra-red, auto-pilots and transmission equipment – the words ran in a jumble through Hazel's mind. She could think of nothing to say.

The silver girl sighed. "You have strange ways on your planet, but we were warned. I should not be here at all . . ." she stopped with a frown and then continued, "Perhaps it is the language, though I passed with honours from the radio-broadcast language centre."

The girl untwisted herself and paced about the floor. She wound herself about a pole that ran from the curved ceiling to the curved floor. She hung there with her eyes closed, apparently deep in thought.

Then she opened her eyes and said, "Of course, I haven't introduced myself!" She uncoiled herself and said, "You must call me Aislinn; that is the closest I can get in translation."

Hazel said, "This isn't all a joke? You've come here in this thing people can't see from the outside, all by yourself and from some strange place?"

"Planet," Aislinn said, "and this is my spaceship. Though perhaps it will not be for much longer."

Hazel could hardly believe it: a girl from another planet, a girl who was no bigger than Hazel herself. And this girl drove, or rode, or was it flew, a spaceship? "But why," she said, "mightn't you have your spaceship much longer?"

"If I fail I shall have to decompose it," the girl said.

"Decompose?"

Aislinn said, "You don't understand? I shall have to make it as though it had never been."

"You mean if you don't get those things mended?"

"Mended in time to contact my people so that I can join them on the mission," Aislinn said. "Will you help?"

Hazel felt very weak. She clutched at a metal panel that projected slightly from one curving wall. She was not dreaming, it was quite solid. What would Simon and John think? "Simon and John!" said Hazel.

"You have two names?" Aislinn said.

"No. I'm Hazel. Simon's my cousin and John's his friend." Hazel was glad to have the firm panel beneath her hands.

"The dim creatures?" Aislinn said.

Hazel pushed herself upright. "Simon's not dim," she said, "it's just that he's slower at maths than I am."

Aislinn wound herself about the chair. 'That *is* bad. He should get his mentor corrected. But I did not mean his maths. I meant that he is one of those people with a dim beam."

Mentors and maths, people with dim beams! Hazel's thoughts began to spin. She decided not to explore those things now and said, "Simon'll be feeling more than dim if he has to go home without me. You'll have to let me out to tell him and John."

"Not necessary," Aislinn said, "they are quite safe. I will activate the viewing screen and show you. Look."

She flipped a switch on the panel. Light shone in a small screen and a faint picture appeared. It was the playground at dusk. Hazel could see the figures of Simon and John. They stared directly at her.

It was a moment or two before Hazel realized how still the picture was. Simon and John stood awkwardly. Their arms and legs were stiff like some figures she had once seen in a waxworks museum.

"You see," Aislinn said, "they are quite safe."

"What's happened to them? I must get out and see."

Aislinn touched the switch and the screen went blank. "There's nothing to worry about. You can stay here and talk to me."

Hazel beat with her fists on one of the curved metallic walls. "What have you done to them. Let me out!"

"Please be tranquil," Aislinn said. "How can you help me if your metabolism goes wrong?"

Hazel's fists were sore. She stopped her beating. Instead she studied the wall. There was not even a slight crack that indicated a hidden door or sliding panel. She turned to face Aislinn. "I must know what's happening."

Aislinn sat calmly in the chair. "I suppose your people are not used to different dimensions," she said thoughtfully.

"What I want to know," Hazel said, "is why Simon and John aren't moving if they're all right."

"I had only enough power left to do it this once," Aislinn said, "but it is because I stretched a moment of time when I invited you in."

"It was a funny sort of invitation," Hazel said, "and I don't know what business you have to be stretching bits of time."

"I showed you friendship," Aislinn said, "by reflecting your own appearance back at you. I led you to my spaceship. At great risk I invited you in. And now all you want to do is leave and see to the dim creatures."

Hazel was silent.

"Don't go," Aislinn said. "I'm quite alone until I can contact my people's mission control again."

Hazel asked, "Don't I have to stay if you won't let me out?"

Aislinn appeared to droop. "I cannot keep you here if you feel so strongly about leaving. It is against our custom to restrain aborigines."

Aborigines, Hazel thought! Aloud she said, "I'll stay if you'll let Simon and John come in too."

Aislinn darted off the chair and shrank back against the instrument panel. "They will not bring weapons?"

"Weapons?"

Aislinn held something towards Hazel, she held it stiffly as though afraid it could bite.

"So you have got the boomerang," Hazel said.

"I had to disarm them," Aislinn said. "I have tested this and it is not nuclear, but I must be sure they will bring no weapons in with them."

"That's a sort of toy," Hazel said, "we haven't any real weapons."

Aislinn pushed the boomerang behind her with

an expression of distaste. "Very well, they may come in if you will vouch for them."

She motioned to one of the chairs. "Please sit down and do not be afraid when I use the infra-red. Its radiations are quite harmless."

The warmth increased. Walls and ceiling glowed with the reddish light. The humming of the panel grew. One wall seemed to dissolve and the two boys stumbled in.

CHAPTER FIVE

"*How* far did you say it is to this Alpha whatsit place?" John said.

"Alpha Centauri A is the name of the system and my planet is Spiralmetra," Aislinn said. "It is only 4.3 light years; we are quite close neighbours."

"Close neighbours!" John said. "But a beam of light travels thousands of miles a second – it must be millions of miles . . ."

"Trillions," Aislinn said.

John looked doubtfully at Aislinn. "You must be having us on. Nobody can travel in space like that."

"*This* is no joke," Simon said. He was prowling up and down before the instrument panel.

"Think of how you came in here," Hazel said to John. "We couldn't see this spaceship from outside, but it is here."

"Well, how do they do it then?" John said.

"We have found the way to transmit matter intact by slipping through another space/time continuum."

John tugged his left ear for a moment. Then he said, "I don't see how we can help. If Aislinn can whizz through space like that, her people must be miles ahead of us in science. What could *we* do?"

Hazel studied John as he squatted on the floor. Then her eyes turned to Simon, who stood entranced in front of the murmuring instrument panel.

Since he had recovered from the shock of entering an invisible spaceship, Simon had hardly taken his eyes from the many switches and rippling lights. He said now, "This is a bit of all right."

John said, "I think we ought to tell the space research people, or the police or someone. Then they could help."

"No!" Although Aislinn was small, her angry voice filled the cabin. "Not your authorities; none of your space research people."

"Why not? It's only common sense," John said.

"I only landed in emergency!" Aislinn cried. "I could destroy the spaceship completely and it would be better for me to do that than make my presence known to your people. Why do you think I did not contact anyone until I found Hazel, who has the true beam? Why do you think we of Alpha Centauri have avoided your planet for so long?"

"Keep your hair on," Simon said.

Hazel saw John wince at Aislinn's fury and she said, "Aislinn did say it was just some wiring.... I thought..."

Aislinn's crystal eyes softened. "It is the wiring of the mentor which directs the self-repair unit that must be mended. Then I can send a beam to my people. They will send information from their all-seeing mentor, so that my mentor can instruct the self-repair unit how to correct the matter transmission equipment."

"Mentor?" John said.

Simon turned unwillingly from the instrument panel. "Like a computer."

"But why can't *you* do it?" John asked Aislinn. "If your people are so clever as to dash about space so that you can't be seen or heard, why can't you repair your own spaceship?"

"It is impossible for us," Aislinn said, "we can operate machines and equipment, but never the parts that actually make them work."

"Somebody must do those things on your planet," John said.

"The robots do," Aislinn said. "Our robots never travel in space nor do our Great Thinkers, but my people do. Once my people used to see to machines, but when we learned to move in space in this different way, we found we could not do any mechanics – all our equipment went wrong and there were many accidents."

"Like some people always make watches go wrong," Simon said.

John whistled softly to himself. "You mean you can whizz from planet to planet, but you couldn't repair a plug?"

Aislinn had turned away so that her face was hidden. She was silent.

John stared at her. Then he said, "I've got it – that's why you landed here, that's how your spaceship went wrong. You touched something!"

"I am ashamed," Aislinn said, "I worked out a way to switch over the auto-pilot so that I could guide the ship myself. I only had to cross over two tiny pieces of wire. I came down towards your planet, just to look not to land. They had told us so much I was curious. . . . and then . . ."

"Well!" John said.

"It was a terrible thing to do," Aislinn said. "And now the power is too low for me to leave your planet's atmosphere by manual control and the automatic equipment is jammed. The mother ship is on its way to Eridanus and I have endangered all our security. I have failed on my first mission."

"Sounds a right old secret service do," said Simon in some awe.

Aislinn said, "Unless I can rejoin my people I deserve only scorn."

John was beginning to look more sympathetic. "I don't know, it makes you kind of human – almost."

"I'd have a bash at helping," Simon said.

Hazel saw his eyes return to the instrument panel in fascination. She said to John, "We could at least help her to move to another place for safety."

Simon said, "Who's going to catch on while she's fitted up with this invisible caper?"

"*And* she can fix people like she fixed us," John said.

"I saw shapes," Hazel said, "not anything definite, but they were there – a sort of glimmer."

Aislinn sighed. "The force field power that makes the ship invisible is fading, that is why Hazel saw the glimmer. When the power goes I shall no longer be able to protect the ship by 'fixing' people, as John calls it."

"It's like a run-down battery," Simon said.

Aislinn nodded. "I had to waste energy. First of all I landed on a most uncomfortable place, where large, rumbling machines roared in and out. There were many people."

"Sounds like a railway station," John said.

"Then I moved to a place where there were smaller machines which stopped and traded and then went on again. The mentor registered explosives."

"Petrol," Simon said, "she must have landed on a garage."

"It's a marvel nothing crashed into that force field thing," John said.

"So eventually, I came here where there are young ones. I thought it would be necessary to decompose the ship unless I got help soon."

"You mean blow it up? There'd be a right old do if you did it here," Simon said with something like relish.

"And," John said, "you can't get away from our earth either unless you mend that mentor thing."

"So," Hazel said, "Aislinn wants somewhere safe and quiet. Somewhere without people around all day."

"All right, I give in," John said, "we'll have to help. But where? The only place I can think of is Grainsby Tower."

"That might do," Hazel said, "there aren't any woods near the town she could hide in, only flat fields where you could see the glimmer for miles."

"She'd be half-hidden on top of that tower," Simon said.

"And if there was a glimmer, people would just think old Charlie was on one of his midnight trails."

Aislinn looked from one to the other. "Grainsby Tower, old Charlie? Please explain."

"Grainsby Tower's an ancient monument," Hazel said, "only hardly anybody goes in to see it, specially in the winter. Charlie Kinnick's the warden, he looks after it."

"Everyone thinks he's bats," Simon said.

"He wanders about looking for his ghosts," said Hazel.

"Ghosts?" Aislinn asked.

"Oh, spirits, people that are sort of half-alive," Hazel said, and she thought how she had believed Aislinn was a ghost such a short while ago.

"It's a brainwave," John said excitedly, "no one'd take any notice if old Charlie started to talk about anything odd."

Hazel feared that Aislinn might take offence at the use of the word 'odd', but the silver girl seemed quite unperturbed. Aislinn went across to the instrument panel. "There is enough power for only one more low-flying journey. But I will risk it on your advice. Direct me, please."

"She trusts us," Hazel thought, as she watched Simon take a stub of pencil and an old envelope from his pocket. He started to draw a rough map.

"Here's the school. That the main street. The tower's past the cemetery, and before you get to the flour mill. It's next to the rugby field. The straight way by air's over the Minster, but you'll have to go up three hundred feet."

It was the longest speech Hazel had ever heard Simon make.

Aislinn checked a switch. "Three hundred feet."

Simon frowned over his map, putting in arrows and marking high buildings with crosses. Hazel reflected that she wouldn't have known where to start such directions. She hadn't realised before that Simon's fascination with aerial photographs and maps would be useful one day.

"Please be prepared for the infra-red," Aislinn said.

There was a faint whirr. Hazel had the sensation of being in a lift. Her stomach lurched as the craft took off.

CHAPTER SIX

It seemed that they travelled above another world. It was a world where the sky and water were black and the buildings and an occasional tree brilliant white.

Hazel looked down through the narrow, curved observation slit and saw the darkening earth speed away from them in a blur. She heard Simon say,

"Up a bit more," and her inside lurched again as the spaceship lifted over the elegantly fluted top of the Minster. Hazel decided that the Minster now looked rather like a cake-decoration.

As dusk deepened more completely into night, they came nearer to the ground. The lights of Ros-thorpe gathered together to make a reddish glow. The afterglow of car exhausts left trails along the roads and in the sky remained the warm path of a jet aeroplane which had passed long ago.

To Hazel it felt as though they were in the midst of some wonderful adventure. It was like the open-ing of a doorway into an unimagined universe.

Simon was whistling. Suddenly his whistling stopped. "Not much for the pilot to see, is there?" The front of the ship had no screen through which to look ahead.

"It is not necessary," Aislinn said, "the infra-red sensing devices seize on the given target."

Hazel could see nothing clearly in the cabin. Simon and Aislinn were two indistinct shapes by the instrument panel, which shone as though it were alive. John was a vague hump by the opposite ob-servation slit. Hazel heard the click of a switch. She felt a soft bump. The dimness slowly returned to golden white.

Aislinn patted the instrument panel kindly, al-most as one might a live creature. "A satisfactory journey," she said.

"We did it," Simon said. His face had the blissful look it usually wore when he had just eaten an ice-cream.

John, on the other hand, looked as though he had eaten something quite unpleasant. He was paler than usual.

"Have you landed properly then?" Hazel said.

"Naturally," Aislinn said, "but now, if you are to help, all three of you will have to be tested."

"Tested?" Hazel said.

"How can you test us?" John said. "We don't know anything about spaceships."

"I don't mind – if it's not like school tests," Simon said.

"It is simple," Aislinn said. "I must find out first of all that the equipment will not hurt you, nor you the equipment. Then I must know which one of you can most satisfactorily carry out the repair. We will try Hazel first."

Hazel found herself motioned towards the machine by the instrument panel which Aislinn had called her "mentor". Aislinn directed her to hold a bar in both hands. The humming of the instrument panel stopped abruptly.

"Look at the blue eye in the mentor," Aislinn said.

The blue eye seemed to probe through Hazel's spectacles and into her eyes. Abstract images danced before her. Hazel felt a wave of vibration.

"That is all," Aislinn said, "now John."

Hazel stepped away and watched John and Simon in their turn grasp the bar and blink at the blue eye. When they had finished, something like ticker tape whirled from a slot in the mentor.

"Now you must return to your people," Aislinn

said. "When you visit me again I shall know who is to do the work."

"Perhaps we all could," John said.

"It is unlikely. Remember what Simon said about watches, and then think that this equipment is a hundred times more delicate than the mechanism of a watch."

"Supposing your machine picks the wrong one?" Hazel said. "I don't know anything about wires."

"It will choose correctly," Aislinn said. Then she indicated a large, gleaming switch to one side of the instrument panel. "One warning: this switch must on no account be touched by any of you. The mentor cannot test reaction to it."

Hazel glanced at the switch. She saw that Aislinn had left the blue plastic boomerang lying to one side of it. She said, "We'll come back as soon as we can tomorrow."

"You will respect my secrecy?" Aislinn said.

"Duncan might be suspicious," Hazel said, "if he doesn't get his boomerang back. Shall I take it for him?"

Aislinn sighed. "I suppose it would be safer. Your civilisation seems so primitive."

"Primitive, she says!" John laughed, but there was an angry note in his voice. "*You* still have breakdowns, and you're not above asking us for help."

"Stuff it!" Simon said. "That's just the way she talks."

"My words offend you?" Aislinn said. "I only express facts as they were taught to me. Hazel understands, I think; she has the true beam."

"Proper ray of sunshine, that's her," Simon said.

"I don't know what you mean by beams, anyway," John said.

Aislinn touched her forehead. "It is something from here. It is a kind of light. When it is there clearly it composes many things."

John had stuck his hands in his coat pocket and was scowling. He did not look at Aislinn. Hazel was embarrassed and she felt a rush of relief when Simon winked at her.

He said, "Let's get off home before her head's too swollen to get in Aunt Edna's front door."

John appeared a little more pleased. "Tomorrow afternoon?" he said.

Aislinn looked at him, a puzzled line between her eyes. Hazel believed that the spacegirl truly did not understand why John took offence at certain words, or that John should be ill at ease when Hazel was praised. But still Aislinn said, "I place my trust in the three of you."

Her voice faded as the hidden force propelled the three children through the apparently melting side of the spaceship.

"No one should find her there," John said.

The children looked upwards to the tower battlement from the balcony below.

Hazel said, "There's a glimmer!" But the glimmer flickered briefly and then went out. The tower top was once more dark and empty against the night sky.

The children ducked under the archway to the inside stairs. They had to feel their way down carefully in the pitch-black interior, clutching at the uneven, knotted rope that served as a rail. They came to the foot of the tower, out into the open and looked up again at the battlement.

"Old Charlie's ghost will have a shock if it comes out tonight," John said.

"Could ghosts get a shock?" Hazel said. "It might walk right through the force field and the ship as well."

"Old Charlie'd get the shock," Simon said.

"He wouldn't know what to make of it anyway," John said.

It was very quiet. The children crept past the light in old Charlie's small cottage, then ran by the wooden shed. The entrance gate was locked and so they climbed over the flint-topped wall.

They dusted down their clothes beneath the street lamp outside. John stared at the notice board that read:

"Grainsby Tower – Scheduled for Preservation as an Ancient Monument.

Admission: Adults 5p. Children 2p.

Hours of Admission: 11 a.m. to dusk."

"Have you thought," John said, "that we'll have to pay to get in?"

"There's ways and means," said Simon darkly.

John moved uneasily. "It's not as simple as I thought at first. Too many things could happen. We ought to do things to stop people finding out – from going up to look at the tower at all."

"Like what?" Simon said.

They heard the Minster clock chime nine faintly across the town.

"We've done what we can," Hazel said, "and if we're any later tonight my Mum won't let us come tomorrow."

John said, "I suppose hanging on won't make it better."

The children ran beneath the street lamps towards home. It was not until they had parted from John and reached the Bradley's front door that Hazel realised she had forgotten to bring Duncan's boomerang.

CHAPTER SEVEN

"I'm not at all sure," said Mr. Bradley, "that either you or Simon ought to be allowed out after your behaviour last night."

"I can't think what got into Hazel," Mrs. Bradley said, "I know she's forgetful sometimes, but it's not like her at all to miss Guides and go off playing rough with Simon and John."

"Your mother nearly had the police out when you weren't home at nine o'clock," Mr. Bradley said.

It was Saturday and they had just finished dinner. Mr. Bradley was poking at his pipe to remove the old, burnt tobacco.

"Don't do that at the table, Jim," Mrs. Bradley said. She began to scrape the dirty plates and stack them together.

"We'll do the washing up, Mum," Hazel said, "won't we, Simon?"

Mr. Bradley got up to look for his large ashtray. "Anything to get round us, eh?"

"Well, at least they're trying to be helpful now, Jim," Mrs. Bradley said. "Where did you say you want to go?"

"Grainsby Tower," Simon said.

"It's educational – historic," said Hazel.

"First time I've known either of you want to go anywhere educational or historic," Mr. Bradley said, but his voice told Hazel that he was weakening.

Hazel pulled Simon's sleeve to get him into the kitchen. She was in a hurry to get to the tower and angry because she had forgotten the boomerang last night. She thought perhaps she could put things right if they got to the tower quickly.

"John's late," Simon said, "we hung about at the gate, but old Charlie's eyes were popping so we came on."

Aislinn nodded calmly as though such things were matter of course. But Hazel, knowing how John was always on time, was uneasy in her mind; she stared at the boomerang.

Her thoughts were interrupted by Aislinn, who said swiftly, "I have the results of the testing. Simon is the most suitable one to do the repair, and it will be safe for him to do so. It is good news. He must start immediately."

Simon had flopped against the projecting panel Now he jerked to attention. "Me?"

"Aislinn. . . ." Hazel began, thinking of the boomerang, but she stopped when the silver girl lifted her hand imperiously.

Aislinn beckoned to Simon. He approached the instrument panel with a look of rapt attention on his face. Aislinn placed a large sheet covered in diagrams before him, and unrolled a layer of crinkly substance which she placed on the floor. She pointed to the sheet. "These are your instructions."

Simon nodded briefly. He took his small screwdriver from his pocket and unscrewed the section Aislinn pointed out to him. He lifted off the unscrewed section. His eyes shone, and then he frowned.

"There's your trouble," he said, reminding Hazel of the plumber who had come last year to see about the clunking noise the water pipes made.

Within the section Simon had revealed was a twisted mass of blackened wires. He said, "This wire's all burnt out. Have to be stripped down. Funny it don't look like the computer pictures I've seen."

Aislinn started to say, "I will ask the mentor what. . . ." when she was interrupted by a red light flashing on the panel. She flicked the viewing switch and the screen lit to show the bottom of the tower.

Hazel saw John running across the grass. Behind him pounded Duncan.

John reached the steps. He stopped and turned. He seemed to be arguing with Duncan.

"I should have taken the boomerang," Hazel thought. Aloud she said, "What do we do now? He's followed John to get the boomerang."

"Nosey-parkering more like," Simon said. "Throw the boomerang out, that'll keep him quiet."

"This," Aislinn said, as she held out the blue plastic boomerang, "belongs to the dim creature with the red face?"

"Duncan'd do his nut, if he heard you call him dim," Simon said.

"Aislinn doesn't mean dim like we do," Hazel said. "Can we throw it out, Aislinn?"

Duncan had grasped John's arm and was twisting it. The two boys tussled.

Aislinn pressed the switch and then tossed the boomerang through the dissolving wall. On the

screen they saw the flight of the boomerang. It curved out away from the tower, but lifted before it reached the gound.

Hazel held her breath. Aislinn had made the

boomerang work. It flicked over with a twisting movement and rose up again almost in slow motion. Duncan stopped his struggle with John and stared at the boomerang.

The boomerang came whizzing back into the spaceship cabin. Aislinn caught it neatly. Hazel saw that John took advantage of Duncan's amazement to dart away. Duncan recovered and dashed after him.

Aislinn looked at the boomerang with renewed interest. "It is a neat weapon," she said, "but not, I think, one to use often." She placed it carefully beside the forbidden switch once more.

"What now?" said Simon. "They'll both be up here in a jiffy."

"The time dilation effect is exhausted. I have no alternative but to let them both in," Aislinn said, "much as I deplore an overcrowded spaceship." She dissolved the wall.

John came flying into the cabin at a tremendous speed. Duncan catapulted in behind him.

"So, this is the very dim creature," Aislinn said, as she activated the switch and returned them to normal light and heat.

"Not 'dim', Aislinn," Hazel said.

"Ah, I had forgotten!" Aislinn studied the astonished Duncan, who was sprawled against the now solidly curving wall.

"In any case," Aislinn said, "it was an inaccuracy. This creature has a very strong beam, but it is all confused. It flashes on and off."

"That's Duncan all right," Simon said.

"But what shall we do with him?" Hazel said.

"We could tie him up," said John.

"Such hostility is not necessary," Aislinn said, "we must explain to him."

"You needn't talk about me as if I wasn't here," Duncan said, almost in a gasp. "What *is* this? A joke? And there's my boomerang – I knew you'd got it, Hazel Bradley."

"He was after me for it," John said. "I thought I'd shaken him off, but he turned up again when I'd paid old Charlie."

Simon glowered at Duncan and said, "He'd better watch himself now he's here."

Some time later Duncan said, "I don't believe it."

"Well, you've got to believe your own eyes, haven't you?" John said.

"It's all solid," Hazel said, "and Aislinn, she's quite real."

"Simon working away at those wires, you two standing guard and a visitor from outer space – nobody would believe me if I told them, would they?" Duncan said.

"You'd better not tell," John said, "we've all given our word. So you just mind out."

Hazel said, "But now you're in on it you won't want to tell, will you?"

Duncan looked round the cabin, as though trying to weigh everything up. "If I'm in on it . . . well . . ."

Hazel watched him hopefully. She could not

think what they would do if Duncan decided he was not with them. It would be in some way her fault, after all.

Duncan continued, "I'd be a fool to tell, wouldn't I?"

From the instrument panel, Simon said, "That's it, 'til there's new wire." A mass of blackened wires lay on the floor.

Aislinn got up from her seat in front of the instrument panel. She opened a small chute by pressing a button. "Please put the burnt wires into the destructor, Simon." She handed Simon a strip of paper.

He took it and whistled. "Coo – more stuff as well as copper wire!"

John went across to look at the list. Hazel was about to join him when she saw Duncan sidle to the other end of the instrument panel. His hand reached out to the boomerang.

"Duncan," Hazel said, "we mustn't touch that switch!" She saw his hand drop to his side and he turned away.

Hazel stood peering over John's shoulder to study the list. Like Simon she could understand about the copper wire, but she was puzzled by the large magnet and the iron filings. "Where shall we get them?" she said.

"Where's your good little Girl Guide spirit?" said John.

"There's ways and means," Simon said.

"Tomorrow then," John said to Aislinn as Simon slipped the list into his pocket. "We'll have to come after dinner – people always make such a fuss about roast beef on Sunday. What's up, Duncan?"

Duncan stood by the projecting panel. His face was very pale. He clutched the boomerang tightly.

"Tired," said Duncan in a mumble, "it was all that heat."

The children stood outside the tower in the fading afternoon light. Duncan sat on the bottom step of the tower, his head between his hands, and Hazel watched him with concern.

"I feel sick," he said.

The boomerang lay at Duncan's feet and Hazel picked it up. "He might tell."

"No," Duncan said.

"Why should he?" John said. "Wouldn't do him any good."

"I don't think he will," Hazel said, "but. . . ." she stared at Duncan, not knowing how to put her feeling into words.

Duncan lifted his head. He looked in front of him stiffly as though sleepwalking. He stood up and walked forward.

"Go with him, Simon . . . John," Hazel pleaded, "and I'll go home and ask them to wait tea."

"Perhaps it's that blooming, flashing beam of his," Simon said, as he and John set off to follow Duncan.

Old Charlie peered out from the wooden shed that was his office. "Owd tower's doin' fine today," he said in his wheezy voice, "shall you be comin' back? 'appen you'll see my ghost."

Hazel watched the boys turn in the opposite direction from the Bradley's house. Duncan was so pale; he walked so stiffly. Had he touched that switch, she wondered?

CHAPTER EIGHT

"Stop fussing about Duncan," John said to Hazel.

It was Sunday afternoon and the children were in Mr. Bradley's garden shed. Before them was a cardboard box, over which Simon brooded.

"But he looked so odd," Hazel said, "not like Duncan at all."

"Huh!" Simon said. "Who says Duncan's not odd? Hope John's magnet's big enough, whatever Aislinn wants it for."

"It's the best we can do on Sunday," John said.

Simon said, "Take me years to save up that much copper wire again."

"You might listen!" Hazel said. "I think Duncan might have touched that switch."

"Perhaps you have to do more than touch it, like pull it or something, before it hurts you. He was all right when we left him. And you didn't *see* him touch it, did you?" John said.

"But. . . ." Hazel began, to lapse into silence when John lifted his eyebrows in a long-suffering way.

John peered inside the box. "Doesn't seem much to repair a spaceship that changes itself from something to nothing and back again."

"It's an odd lark," Simon said, "but it's all done with the wires. Line 'em up just right, then this juice stuff of theirs flows through."

"Hope you're not mucking around with nuclear energy," John said.

"Nah, more like electric. It's the way they use it turns it into something else."

"We ought to get a move on," Hazel said, "we promised to be there after dinner."

John jumped up. "Synchronise watches," he said.

"You've been watching those old war films," Hazel said.

"It's a good idea to have time checks, anyway," John said. "Where are you two going officially? And how're we going to get this box past your kitchen window without any questions?"

"Slip the box round the side way, then Aunt Edna won't catch on."

"And we're still doing this history project at the tower if Mum wants to know," Hazel said.

As they went down the path to the house, Simon said, "That history thing won't wash for long."

They saw Mrs. Bradley's plump figure outlined against the glass of the back door. John darted out of sight along the side way.

Mrs. Bradley opened the door. Her face was flushed. She stared at Simon and Hazel. "What's this about Duncan?"

"Duncan?" Hazel said, knowing that her voice sounded wobbly.

"Duncan," Mrs. Bradley said firmly. "Mrs. Wright's just rung up. The most peculiar thing has happened – she thought you two might know something about it."

Hazel swallowed hard. "Us? About what?"

"Well, it seems Duncan was babbling about space-ships first of all," Mrs. Bradley said, "now he won't say anything. But he did say he was with you yesterday afternoon and Mrs. Wright thinks it must have started then. What were you doing?"

Simon looked sideways at Hazel and then said, "Larking about, that's all."

"You're sure neither of you were up to anything silly?" Mrs. Bradley frowned at them. "Well, *your* hair looks quite normal."

"Hair?" said Hazel.

"I told Mrs. Wright you wouldn't know anything about it. I knew it all along. Purple hair, indeed!"

"Purple?" Hazel said.

"Purple. That's the colour of Duncan's hair now, his mother says."

"We didn't do nothing," Simon said.

"Anything," said Mrs. Bradley. "But did you ever hear such a thing?"

Hazel said, "Did Duncan's mother say anything else?"

Mrs. Bradley shook her head. "Only that he was going on about space travel. Just what were you up to yesterday afternoon?"

"We've still got Duncan's boomerang," Hazel said carefully, "he'd lost it, you see. You've got it in your pocket, Simon. Shall we take it round to him? It might help."

"It might," Mrs. Bradley said uncertainly, "but I don't see what a boomerang has got to do with purple hair."

"We'll go now then, Simon, shall we?" Hazel jogged Simon's arm.

Simon rummaged in the pocket of his duffle coat and brought out the boomerang.

"I don't know." Mrs. Bradley closed the back door and followed them round the side way. "Don't you go getting mixed up in anything peculiar."

Hazel saw John dart behind one of the large chestnut trees that lined the road outside. One end of the box stuck out from the tree trunk, but her mother appeared not to notice.

"I suppose they'll try to wash it out, the purple I mean?" Hazel said.

Mrs. Bradley bent over to pull off a dead rose bloom. "I suppose they will. Mrs. Wright's sent for the doctor. She doesn't like the look of Duncan at all, she says."

"Who would," Simon muttered.

Hazel watched in fascination as the end of the box wavered. She said, "Those roses need cutting off Mum. Shall we help you when we get back?"

"Not the roses, you mustn't touch those," Mrs. Bradley said. "I'll get the secateurs and do them. You be quick and take that boomerang back if you're set on it."

Mrs. Bradley went round the side of the house and John came out from behind the tree. He signalled to Hazel and Simon and hurried down the road. As they turned to hurry after him, Mrs. Bradley reappeared. "You be careful now. Don't you get involved in Duncan's tricks!"

They heard her slippers flapping on the concrete as she went purposefully towards the garden shed.

"I heard," John said, as they joined him at the corner of the road, "purple hair! Now what?"

CHAPTER NINE

The trouble with being a girl, Hazel decided, was that boys always dashed away on what they considered important matters, while girls were left with the awkward business. So Simon and John had gone to the tower and she had to take the boomerang back.

She studied Duncan and said, "You don't feel ill then?" She took off her glasses to wipe them and the blurriness made the purple of Duncan's hair appear less startling.

"I'm all right," Duncan said. His face grew bright. "You know I'll be quite a case history, that's what the doctor said."

"Duncan, *did* you touch that switch?"

"Touch it? I think it jumped at me!" Duncan said. "It was like an electric shock."

"You could have kept quiet about everything," Hazel said.

"I didn't mean to tell about being with you lot and the spaceship, but it came out all of a sudden."

Hazel put Duncan's boomerang on the bed. "Your Mum gave me a very queer look. She only let me see you because of the boomerang."

"Mum's all right about it now," Duncan said, "but that reporter...."

"Reporter?"

Duncan nodded. "All the neighbours have been

knocking – someone must've 'phoned the 'Gazette' ".

"What did you say?"

"I didn't see him," Duncan said hastily, "Mum sent him off, she doesn't like reporters. And this was the one that wants spicy stories so that he can make his name and get to Fleet Street."

"Spicy stories!" Hazel said. She wanted to rage at Duncan, but a quiet voice inside her said that she was as much to blame as he was.

She said, "You could pretend that you dyed your hair."

"Well . . ." Duncan said, wriggling about on the pillows, "this is all right now that the nagging's stopped. They'd start on at me again if I said I'd dyed my hair."

Hazel could see that "this" implied the stay in bed, the pile of comics to read and the fruit on Duncan's chest of drawers. She said, "If things go wrong – really wrong – Aislinn will have to blow up her spaceship."

"Anyway, it would be a lie," Duncan said.

"You could pretend you dyed it," Hazel said, "and tell the truth afterwards."

There was a pause during which Duncan stared at the ceiling, apparently considering the matter.

Hazel said, "How would you like to be stranded, millions of miles from home, with people all around you thought might be dangerous?" She got up impatiently and went to the door.

At last Duncan said, "I *am* sorry, you know. I can't promise, Mum being what she is, but I'll try."

Hazel had to be content with that. She darted from the room, crept down the stairs and closed the front door quietly as she left. It seemed impolite, but the less she saw of Mrs. Wright the fewer questions would have to be answered.

Grainsby Tower loomed up before her. It was one of the few tall buildings that made a landscape in this flat country.

Hazel noticed that a mist was creeping up by the old derelict mill farther down the banks of the canal. Old Charlie was nowhere to be seen, so Hazel left twopence on the ledge of his wooden office, and then ran.

Inside Aislinn's spaceship, Hazel blinked until her eyes readjusted. Then the switch clicked and the light flooded to its golden yellow.

Aislinn lifted her arm from the switch. She wrapped herself around the pole as Hazel had seen her do once before, then she closed her eyes.

The boys were squatting on the floor. Hazel began, "I saw Duncan . . ."

John interrupted her. "Aislinn's concentrating; we haven't told her about Duncan yet."

"The repair?" Hazel said.

Simon nodded. "Okey-doke so far."

"She's sent out the beam," John said, "and now we're waiting."

" 'Til her lot pick up the signal," Simon said.

A green light flickered above the instrument panel and Aislinn swiftly unwrapped herself from the pole and went across. The light steadied and remained as a green glow. Aislinn pressed several switches at the top of the instrument panel, then pushed some buttons on her mentor. She turned to face the children.

"My people have sighted the beam."

"Just like that!" Simon said.

The green light flickered again and a white ribbon began to click from the mentor. Aislinn studied the ribbon.

"My people wait in the mother ship, orbiting the solar system planet you call Mars. They will dematerialise immediately and proceed towards your earth's atmosphere. They will arrive when your earth has spun on its axis twice. They will wait for one more axis spin, sending a visible green signal for one hour before their departure. I have to join them before the signal goes."

"They don't signal for long, do they?" John said.

Aislinn said, "It is a risk to security even for one hour."

"But the ship's ready now?" Simon said.

"It will be, when the necessary information has been fed from my mentor to the self-repair unit and this has done its work. The work must not be interrupted."

There was a silence. Hazel's eyes misted behind her spectacles. "If things go wrong, you'd have to decompose the spaceship – and not only the spaceship?"

Aislinn said, "Not just the spaceship, Hazel. And on the night I am ready to take off, your people must be kept away from the tower. Only those within a limited range might be hurt, but we cannot take the risk."

"What about Duncan?" John said.

"The confused one? Where is he?"

Hazel told Aislinn about how Duncan had touched the switch, how his hair had turned purple and he had babbled about spaceships.

"But he *is* well?" Aislinn said. "Reactions are unpredictable. To our Great Thinkers a touch of that switch would be fatal. The confused boy is fortunate that his body chemistry is different from theirs."

"Can't you turn his hair back to brown again?" John said. "Then people would think it was all a practical joke."

"I cannot alter the electromagnetic effects by remote control," Aislinn said. "The hair should grow again normally, if he is otherwise unharmed."

"Trust Duncan to blow the gaff," said Simon.

Aislinn looked from one to the other. "Blow the gaff?"

John said, "Split on us."

Hazel said, "They mean tell about the spaceship."

"Then what is to be done?" Aislinn said.

"I've persuaded Duncan to try to pretend he dyed his hair purple," Hazel said.

"And we can trail him," Simon said ominously.

"We could guard the tower," John said.

Aislinn sat on her chair. She folded her hands in her lap, while the instrument panel and the mentor clicked on. She said slowly, "You make me have some admiration for your people, after all."

68

"She don't think so bad of us now," Simon said, as the children went down the stone steps to the balcony.

"But she doesn't think enough of us not to be afraid," John said.

They stopped on the balcony and Hazel said, 'I suppose you know the night they've chosen is Guy Fawkes'?"

"Fireworks and bonfires!" said John.

"Bangers!" Simon said.

"And the display in the rugby field over there," Hazel said.

They stared across from the tower to the rugby field that lay between the tower grounds and the old, derelict mill.

"It's risky," John said.

"We ought to put her wise," Simon said.

Hazel said, "Not now. Look!"

Below in the tower grounds old Charlie was trudging across the damp grass. Two men followed him. One of the men had dark, shiny hair and wore a brown corduroy suit with a yellow, polo-neck shirt. The shorter man looked older and had two cameras slung from straps across his shoulders. The three men went inside the entrance to the tower.

CHAPTER TEN

"I could nip up and put Aislinn wise," Simon said.

"We ought to stay here and put them off," Hazel said.

"Put them off how?" Simon said.

"They might not even be coming because they're suspicious," John said. "Lean against the wall and look as though we don't know anything."

Hazel looked over the parapet wall. It formed a passageway that ran around the four sides of the tower and ended at about her shoulder height.

The men's footsteps clattered nearby and the man with the yellow shirt came on to the balcony first. He looked at the children and said, "Aren't you kids afraid of U.F.O's?"

"You don't care about my ghost," said old Charlie. He caught sight of Hazel. "You 'aven't paid."

"I left the money," Hazel said.

"Everybody's very keen on the tower all of a sudden," old Charlie said. "Only a mention of flying saucers and they can't keep away. I've been telling them about my ghost for years, but do they care?"

"You can save your ghost, Charlie," said the yellow-shirted man. He moved towards the parapet wall and looked over.

The man with the cameras said, "If you ask me, this is a waste of a good Sunday afternoon."

"We don't often get lads in Rosthorpe whose hair

turns purple, *and* rumours about spaceships," said the yellow-shirted man.

"You go-getting cub-reporters make me sick," said the cameraman.

While the two men were talking, Hazel crept across and sat on the second of the steps leading up to the battlement tower. She gestured urgently at Simon and he said to the newspapermen, "You looking for something then?"

The reporter swung round. "Are you kids the ones who were with that lad yesterday?"

"Duncan?" John said. He edged towards the steps and sat down next to Hazel. Simon stood on the other side of her and leaned against the wall. Between them they completely blocked the foot of the steps.

Hazel thought swiftly. It was a big risk, but she gulped and took it. "Have you come to see our spaceship?"

She heard Simon gasp and John utter a wordless exclamation.

Old Charlie glared at her. "Don't you go saying there's space things here," he said, "there's only my ghost. I ought to know, but these smart chaps won't listen to me."

"But you wouldn't see our spaceship," Hazel said, "because we make it invisible. And it's not here; this is our look-out tower. The spaceship's over there." She waved her arm in the direction of the old mill.

"I told you it was a waste of time," the cameraman said to the reporter, "can't you see they're having you on?"

"We can take you over to the mill to inspect it if you like," Hazel said. "I'm sorry we haven't got our space helmets on today, but we're not ready for blast-off yet." She gave fervent thanks to the detailed broadcasts about the Space Programme.

The reporter looked at her steadily. "You kids have got some ideas! What about that lad's purple hair – how do you account for that?"

John seemed to have taken heart at the new situation. He said, "He's the alien, you see. Copper sulphamangachloride is very effective for purple hair."

Hazel looked at him in admiration; she didn't know if there was such a thing as copper sulphamangachloride, but it sounded most impressive. She said, "John's the Captain, you see."

"And who's he?" the reporter said, looking at Simon.

"Computer expert and spaceship technician," John said.

"I mend things," said Simon.

Old Charlie grunted, but the cameraman burst out laughing. "It's a game," he said, "if you can't see that, Jeff, you don't stand much chance of getting to Fleet Street."

"Now I could give you a real ghost story," old Charlie said.

The reporter looked from one to other of the children. "Might be some sort of story in this though."

"Not on your nelly," said the cameraman. "You

can see for yourself there's nothing on this balcony. And can you see anything that looks like a space-ship anywhere else? You couldn't hide one of those. I want my tea, even if you feel like playing space heroes."

The cameraman moved away towards the arch-way to the inside steps and old Charlie followed him.

"Old Charlie doesn't half go on about that ghost," Simon said.

"He doesn't understand the thrill of space travel," John said.

"Jeff!" the cameraman called from the inside steps. "The old boy says he wants to lock up."

Hazel stood up and brushed her skirt. She was quite getting into the flow of the space game con-versation and said, "We've got to go to our space-ship at the mill now."

"The mill, you say?" The reporter stared at Hazel in a bemused way. "You kids go in for these games in a big way."

"We'll have to go if old Charlie's locking up," John said, "he might not let us in to our look-out tower if we get on the wrong side of him."

The reporter turned slowly towards the archway. The children formed a group behind him.

"Keep him on the move," Simon hissed.

They found the cameraman waiting at the gate. Old Charlie peered from his wooden office; he eyed the children grimly, but said nothing.

"Do you want to see our spaceship?" Hazel said to the reporter.

"He's got better sense than that," said the cameraman, "and you kids ought to be on your way home before it gets dark. I've got kids of my own and I wouldn't have them playing around old mills at night."

Hazel heard old Charlie slam the entrance gates behind them and turn the key in the lock. She breathed more easily.

"Off you go home now," said the cameraman. "Come *on*, Jeff."

"Some other time then," said the reporter. He was staring at the children as though there was something he wanted to ask them. But he turned away slowly and walked with the cameraman down the road towards the town.

"That was a right turn up!" Simon said.

"It worked though," Hazel said. She watched the newspapermen; once the reporter looked back, first at them and then at the tower. He shook his head and walked on.

"Kids, indeed!" said John. "What do they think we are, little goats? And I suppose you know we'll have to keep up the game now, else that reporter'll get nosey again if we stop playing it."

Hazel did know. In a small town like Rosthorpe news travelled rapidly in some incredible, mysterious way. She said, "We've only got to give Aislinn three days."

The coming three days were to show Hazel what a very long time seventy-two hours could be.

Duncan made a confession of dyeing his hair,

which backed up Hazel's story. Indeed the story went so well that it almost seemed to Hazel things were going too well, except that it was hard work keeping up the pretence. Simon spent most of his spare time carrying out final adjustments to the wiring under Aislinn's directions.

To make sure that people were kept away from the tower on Guy Fawkes' night seemed an impossibility because of old Charlie. But John had the idea of pooling the remainder of their pocket money to buy the old man a ticket for the fireworks display.

The children thought this had solved the difficulty. On Wednesday morning it became apparent that this ideal solution had aroused Mrs. Bradley's suspicion.

"Lies have no legs," Mrs. Bradley said sharply, as she presided over the breakfast table. "Why did you spend your pocket money on that ticket?"

"People always say to be nice to the old at Christmas," Hazel said, "so why not other times?"

"Poor old stick, needs a bit of life," Simon said.

"You children wouldn't have thought of this if you hadn't been poking around that tower."

"That's it," Simon said, "the poor old geezer's always stuck in that tower place."

"Ah well, I suppose what's done is done!" Mrs. Bradley said. "But what with this and that spaceship game, I don't know what's got into you."

Hazel put down her knife and fork and regarded her remaining piece of egg with distaste. Simon was eating with gusto. She scowled at him, but he grinned amiably.

"Motor bike helmets and boxes painted to be computers, and Duncan dyeing his hair purple," Mrs. Bradley said, "it's all over town. People are saying that children of your age should be past playing games like that."

"This is different," Hazel said.

"Different!" Mrs. Bradley exclaimed. "Peculiar is more like. Why, all the neighbours think you're crazy at eleven years old. I've half a mind to stop you from going to that tower."

"Old Thomas thinks it's a bit of all right," Simon said, quite unconcerned at his aunt's words. "He's started us off on one of these project capers – Space in the Seventies."

"*Mr.* Thomas," Mrs. Bradley said. "Is that so, though? You never know what will take a teacher's fancy!"

"I don't think I like cooked breakfasts before school," Hazel said suddenly. She asked to leave the table and fled the room.

Simon appeared in the hall as she was packing her schoolbag. "You don't have to look so cheerful," she said, "I feel all funny about this evening."

"It'll be O.K.," Simon said. "I tell you, all that stuff in the spaceship is fixed up a treat. Now that magnet and those iron filings, I used for testing. You can get –"

Hazel interrupted him. "It's all right for you, you've been going to the spaceship. John and I have been charging about like six-year-olds, doing countdowns and pretending to look for launching sites."

"Aislinn wants to see *you* before the take-off.

That should cheer you up," Simon said, as they set off for school.

Hazel did not feel cheered. "Pretending Duncan's a creature from outer space!"

Simon said, "Why the cold feet now? We make sure old Charlie's at the fireworks, nip over to the tower and see the ship's O.K. Then bob's your uncle."

"That reporter coming to see Mr. Thomas," Hazel said, "it's wrong somehow."

"He only heard about the project," Simon said.

Perhaps Simon was right, Hazel decided, but she was still uneasy. She thought how when they had met Aislinn it seemed that they were in the midst of a wonderful adventure. Events had changed the wonder.

She would be hopeful, Hazel told herself, and think that all would be well. Tonight would be a chance to recover the feeling and learn something about Aislinn's exotic world.

CHAPTER ELEVEN

Hazel's unease persisted all day and was still with her when darkness grew. Smoke was already penetrating the air when they entered the rugby ground.

The noise of a banger made Hazel jump. She looked at the area where the bonfire was built up; it had been partitioned off with rough fencing. Inside the partition, several men were setting up fireworks and the guy leered at them from a pyramid of kindling.

"Poor old guy," Simon said.

Hazel's eyes searched the crowd for John. She caught a glimpse of him; he was waving both arms rather wildly.

"Mum, can we go over with John?"

"Well..." Mrs. Bradley said.

Hazel said quickly, "We're old enough to keep away from where they let off the fireworks. Look, John's over by the grandstand."

"Let them go, Edna," Mr. Bradley said, "they'll be all right if they're sensible."

"We'll come back soon," Hazel said. She and Simon took advantage of her father's intervention to slip away.

John looked worried. He said, "Let's move back from this crush."

The children pressed backwards through the

crowd. Mrs. Bradley saw them and waved. They waved back dutifully.

"Old Charlie's not here," John said. "I came early and waited at the gate and I've searched and searched."

"We'll have to fetch him," Simon said.

"It'll waste time going there and coming back again," Hazel said.

"Better to waste time than have old Charlie going up the tower," John said.

As a chorus of delight greeted the lighting of a row of golden fountains, the children ran across the field. The mud sucked at their shoes. An orange light flared behind them and they turned to find that the bonfire had been lit.

Hazel stared upwards at the sky and then at the field. She saw two things in rapid succession: a bright green star in the northern sky and an indistinct figure heading in their direction.

She cried, "The signal's in the sky and someone's following us!"

"Over the wall, quick," John said.

They scrambled up the rough stones, caring little for their clothes in the rush, and fell breathless and sticky on the other side.

"Run then!" John said, and they staggered to their feet.

"It's too late," Hazel said.

The figure catapulted down from the wall, almost on top of them. It became mixed up with Simon and they tangled together on the grass.

"Let off!"

Hazel recognised the voice. "It's Duncan."

Simon and Duncan rolled apart and sat up. Duncan gasped and said, "There's something up tonight. You could have let me in on it."

"After the purple hair?" John said. "We've had to play spaceship games for three days solid."

Duncan said, "I've come to help."

"Help!" Simon said.

"Warn you then, about that reporter. He didn't swallow the spaceship game."

"I knew there was something," Hazel whispered.

"He came to see my Mum again this afternoon."

"Did you tell?" John began.

"Course not," Duncan said, "I promised. But he says he's going to have another look at the tower. Going to get old Charlie to take him up there tonight."

"And old Charlie isn't at the display," Hazel said.

Rockets shot up from the rugby field. Hazel looked at the tower; the spaceship glimmered indistinctly. A small light shone from old Charlie's cottage.

"We're sunk," Simon said.

"Not if we stop mooning," John said. "We'll go to the cottage, check up on that reporter and get old Charlie. Hazel must go and see Aislinn and tell her what we're doing."

Through the haze of bonfire smoke that was creeping across the stars, Hazel saw the green signal flickering. "We need a signal for when you get old

Charlie clear and make sure that reporter's not around."

"I've got some sparklers," Duncan said.

John said, "That's it. When all's clear we'll signal to you from the wall with sparklers."

"So little time," Hazel said.

"So we run like mad," John said.

"Sparklers," said Aislinn, "from the wall?" She looked doubtful.

"The boys will wave them about. They do work," Hazel said. She thought that it had been generous of Duncan to give them his sparklers. Although she wondered how the boys were getting on at the cottage, she felt calmer now she was inside the spaceship again.

"Is the spaceship all ready?" she asked.

"Quite ready," Aislinn said, "and the signal is there, as you saw. It is now twenty hundred hours and five minutes by your time; I must leave at twenty hundred hours and fifty minutes at the latest."

Hazel worked out the times to five minutes past eight and ten minutes to nine. The warmth of the spaceship lulled her, but mixed with the contentment was a sadness that Aislinn would leave so soon now. It was as though the door to the whole new world was to be closed without her being able to do more than peep inside.

"So little time," she said, echoing her earlier thought.

Aislinn watched her in silence, and Hazel continued, "I mean for you to tell us about things, about yourself and where you live and – everything. It's all been so rushed."

"But you have my gratitude," Aislinn said.

"We like you." As she said it Hazel wondered whether like was quite the right word. Perhaps what they felt for Aislinn was more like respect mixed with an unsatisfied curiosity.

"It is the kinship," Aislinn said, "you see, I am almost like one of your cousins."

"Cousins?" Hazel said, "but you can't be, not from all those miles away!"

"Listen," Aislinn said, "thousands of years ago, the Great Thinkers of my planet travelled in space themselves. After a journey of many years by conventional space travel, they brought back a few people from your earth. My people have evolved from them. We are almost human, while the Great Thinkers are what you would think of as quite non-human."

"John said you were almost human," Hazel said.

Aislinn said, "But in my people our eyes and skin have developed differently. We are small and very elastic in our movement and we help the Great Thinkers to trade amongst the stars."

"Trade?" Hazel said.

"In many places, and to Epsilon Eridanus. They have a particularly fine piece of music and we have a new poem."

"I thought your mission was. . . ." Hazel began. She had thought Aislinn was some dashing space agent, flying to avert a war or some planetary disaster.

"You could come too," Aislinn said softly.

"Me?"

The green light, which Aislinn had told her mirrored the signal in the sky, flashed suddenly to a great intensity on the instrument panel. Aislinn studied some tape on the mentor, checked switches and finally looked back at Hazel.

"I should like you to come and it would be so easy. My people are still few in number and you would like our life on Spiralmetra."

Hazel stared entranced at the green light. To her surprise she found herself whispering, "New life amongst the distant stars."

"I would take you riding on the winds of space in our gossamer yachts," Aislinn said. "You would learn to travel as I do in hyper-space. You would leave this warlike planet. You would see our Great Thinkers and you would be free."

"Free," Hazel said. How she would love to go.

She stared at the green light. The lens of the viewing screen beside it had passed over old Charlie's cottage. The place was in darkness, so the boys' plan must have succeeded in part. As the lens veered, she saw the sombre tower grounds against the backdrop of the fireworks.

A rocket shot into the air, scattering blue spears. She could be free, like the rocket. They could go within minutes, as soon as the boys signalled from the wall.

"How long before the take-off?" Hazel said.
"Thirty minutes."

Like droplets of shining frost, sparks jumped from the wall. The cluster of sparks moved in an arc, tracing a figure in the air. The figure vanished almost as soon as it was shaped by the sparks, but an after-image was impressed on Hazel's eyes. It was not a figure, but a letter. "H," her mind registered, "A," "Z." She knew it was Simon signalling.

Aislinn turned off the viewing switch and the screen went blank. "The boys' signal, just as you said. We can leave now and will not need the viewing screen again."

Hazel said, "I can't leave my planet, Aislinn."

"You don't want to come?" Aislinn's voice became sharp. "I have sent a message telling my people about you. They are ready to welcome one with such a bright beam."

"I can't," Hazel said, "though I might like your planet."

"I could take off now," Aislinn said, "you would soon forget your life here."

Hazel said, "You wouldn't though, would you; if I didn't want to go?"

Aislinn lifted her hands and then dropped them slowly. She sighed. "There are so few of us. If you want to change your mind I will give you time, I will go at the last possible moment: at twenty hundred hours and fifty minutes."

The cabin light began to fade. "Must *you* go?" Hazel said.

"Yes. You see, I must keep my people's secrets *and* I am part of the poem."

Aislinn put something into Hazel's hand. She became brisk. "Do not be frightened. This is a gift, it will have no bad effects. Perhaps one day, if you understand, we might meet again, in some way or form you do not expect."

Hazel saw Aislinn's shadowy figure against the infra-red of the ship's cabin. Then she was alone on the empty battlement tower, the faint orange glow from the bonfire giving the scene an illusion of warmth.

As Hazel turned towards the stone steps, she looked up at the green signal.

"Star-gazing when there's a bonfire to watch?" said a voice from the shadows.

CHAPTER TWELVE

Hazel stopped in alarm. Then she recognised the voice of the reporter and jumbled plans chased through her mind.

She could see the dim hump of the canal embankment. She heard cries from the crowd as more rockets shot above their heads. She said faintly, "The stars are very interesting."

The reporter came forward from the shadows. "Obviously, but I'm more interested in what's going on around here."

Hazel said, "It's all part of the game. I've got to get to the others in the rugby field."

"And set off to your spaceship at the mill, I suppose?" the reporter said. "I can see that glimmer up there. Old Charlie wouldn't let me in to the tower tonight, but I saw the lads cart him off to the fireworks. *And* I saw you slip inside the tower and up the steps. When I got to the top there was no one here."

Hazel saw that the glimmer was very strong now. And it made a shape rather like an oversize dumbbell. Beyond the glimmer there was faint movement.

"I waited," said the reporter, "and just after someone started waving sparklers on that wall, you came out from nowhere. Don't tell me this is all part of a game. I want to know what you kids have been up to."

The fireworks had ceased, although the bonfire still glowed. Faintly the Minster clock chimed from across the town. Hazel realised that it was half-past eight and there were only twenty minutes to go.

Her jumbled plans resolved into two possibilities. She could try to stop the reporter investigating by telling him the whole story, or she could return to the spaceship and go with Aislinn. The reporter's voice roused her.

". . . and she was saying there's no such thing as copper sulphamangachloride. That's how I got suspicious again and you'd got everything too pat, I thought." He stood blocking Hazel's way to the inside stairs.

The easiest thing would be to return to the spaceship, Hazel decided. The reporter could not follow. Aislinn would be pleased and they would take off like one of the rockets, or perhaps like a bird, or even in some way Hazel had never dreamed of.

"She's an undergraduate – doing science at university," the reporter continued, "so she ought to know. You might as well tell me the whole story."

"Who's a science graduate?" Hazel said, balancing herself for a sudden start towards the glimmer.

"Undergraduate – I told you, my sister. She came home for half-term. I've no head for science – never have had – but Eileen says. . . ."

"What time is it?" Hazel said suddenly. She could see the reporter's face dimly. She thought in amazement, "That reporter is people, I never thought of that. He's got a family and he's curious. He wouldn't just go off if I vanished again, he'd stay right here poking around."

"Time?" the reporter said. "What on earth. . . .?" But he automatically lifted his arm. "Can't really see in these shadows." He took a step towards the bonfire side of the parapet.

Hazel's dream of spaceship travel had collapsed. She must get the reporter away. This seemed the only chance, if it worked. She darted forward. She jolted against the reporter.

"We've got to get off the tower. Radiation!"

The reported clutched at the wall to keep his balance and Hazel ran past him shouting, "Follow me if you want the story!"

She dived under the archway to the inside stairs and heard him cry out, "Where's that child gone?"

"Come on, if you want the story!" Hazel called. She pounded down the dark stairs as fast as she dared.

She halted momentarily. The reporter's footsteps thumped after her and she ran on. Once she heard him stumble in the darkness. He cursed and then started down again.

She came out into the tower grounds and ran across the grass. Her heart beat painfully and her breath came in great gasps.

Hazel paused at the gate with a sigh of relief. The boys had left it unlocked. She checked that the reporter was still following and ran again, guessing that there must be less than five minutes left.

Near the entrance to the rugby ground she

slowed. The reporter's flagging steps were still behind her. He caught up with her and said:

"You're a better sprinter than I am, but you wouldn't make a long distance runner."

Three figures waited inside the entrance to the rugby field. John said, "You been trying to see what's it like being anti-matter?"

"Aislinn said there wasn't no atomic radiation," Simon said, but there was a clear look of relief on his face at the sight of Hazel.

"Well, hurry up then," John said, "let's get farther off so we can see it properly."

"See what?" said the reporter. "If this is another of your tricks..."

"Tricks...." Simon began indignantly, but he never finished the sentence.

Air rushed down. White light reduced the bonfire glow to insignificance. The world around Hazel expanded into another universe in the pureness of the light.

Slowly the white light faded. Hazel became part of the earth again. The four children and the reporter stood shivering on the wet rugby field.

Someone close to the bonfire shouted, "That was a terrific rocket!"

"She went all right," Duncan said.

"It's a success," John said flatly, "she's gone now."

"And all our senses too," said the reporter. "Will somebody please tell me what all this is about?"

"The spaceship game," Simon said.

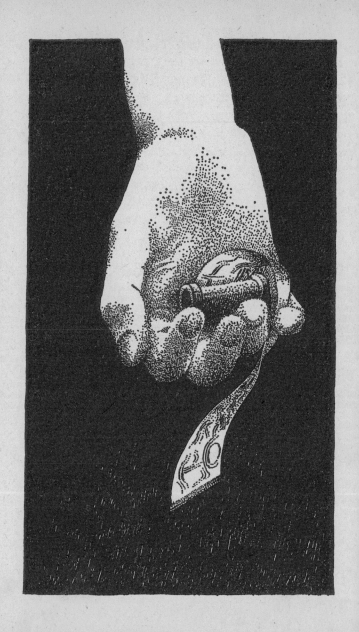

The reporter groaned. "I spotted the flaws in that smartish. Let's have the truth now."

"It's a long story," John said, "let's get warm near the bonfire."

Hazel and Simon walked in front of the others. He listened to her story and said, "All that hoo-haa for a bit of poetry."

"She gave me this." Hazel unclasped her hand, it was stiff from the tight clenching. In her palm was a small, tightly wound scroll. Hazel unrolled it a little. In the bonfire's glow they saw that it was covered with hieroglyphics that ran like spiders.

"What is it?" Simon said.

"Their writing, of course," Hazel said. "I don't think we could read it. It might be one of their poems."

"Looks like Chinese to me," Simon said.

The two children were silent. Above their silence John's voice rose, "You see, what happened was that there was this ghost, cruelly tormented. It was in the old days. . . .'

"Don't give me that," the reporter said.

"No, honest! There's old Charlie – he'll tell you."

Simon looked at the sky. He shook his head. "All those millions of blooming miles for a poem."

"Perhaps," Hazel said, "it wouldn't seem far if we could understand the poem."

DANNY DUNN TIME TRAVELLER
by Jay Williams and Raymond Abrashkin   25p

552 52005 5   Carousel Fiction

Inventions and experiments always fascinated Danny Dunn, but somehow anything of a scientific nature had a habit of going wrong as soon as Danny managed to get himself involved. Professor Bullfinch had a new machine, a machine to challenge the boundaries of TIME itself. Danny was determined not to be left out, unfortunately for the Professor.

TRUE MYSTERIES *by Bob Hoare*   25p

552 54009 9   Carousel Non-Fiction

Tales of the unknown, stories of people who suddenly appear and disappear without explanation, and strange events which present no logical answer, sometimes turning legend into fact, or fact into legend. And always leaving a question mark.

JASON *by Joyce Stranger*   20p

552 52004 7   Carousel Fiction

The pup wasn't wanted, born of a golden Labrador bitch and a giant mastiff. Then Duncan found him, a lonely young boy who needed a friend just as much as Jason needed a loving owner. The closeness between them was only strengthened when Duncan was sent away to school, and then his father had an accident. Jason had to do something.

THE CHILDREN OF TOTEM TOWN
by Kaj Himmelstrup   25p
552 52001 2   Carousel Fiction

A carved totem pole stood sentry over their wooden village,
Tonacatecutli, the Mexican god of creation. But the children's hut village was to be turned into a council car park.
Could the god's influence be called upon to stop the bull-
dozers, even now edging forward to demolish Totem Town?

HAVELOK THE WARRIOR *by Ian Serraillier*   20p
552 52007 1   Carousel Fiction

These are the days when evil men conspired to overthrow the
monarchy, greedy for the power and wealth of wearing the
crown and ruling the land. The King of Denmark is dead,
his son Havelok forced to flee the murderous attempts of
Earl Godard by escaping to the shores of England. He
grows up to be a great warrior, to recover his kingdom.

THE STORY OF BRITAIN *by R. J. Unstead*   30p each
552 54001 3   Carousel Non-Fiction
552 54002 1
552 54003 X
552 54004 8

A country is forged by its history, the battles and intrigues
of by-gone ages laying the foundation of today. From its
beginning as an island to the end of the Second World War,
this series is the record of the men and women who played a
role in shaping the character of England now. It traces the
emergence of England as a nation.

CAROUSEL FICTION PAPERBACK SERIES

HOW AND WHY—WONDER TITLES

All these books are available at your bookshop or newsagent or can be ordered direct from **TRANSWORLD PUBLISHERS**. Just tick the titles you want and fill in the form below.

....

TRANSWORLD PUBLISHERS. Cash Sales Department, P.O. Box 11, Falmouth, Cornwall.

Please send cheque or postal order—no currency, and allow 5p per book to cover the cost of postage and packing.

NAME ....

ADDRESS..

(SEPT/71) ....